For Caitlin, Keith and Devin
who aren't ever tired

GOOD NIGHT

Library of Congress Cataloging in Publication Data: Boynton, Sandra. Good night, good night. SUMMARY: A boatload of animals gets ready for bed, and two rabbits sing them to sleep. 1. Children's stories, American. [1. Bedtime—Fiction. 2. Sleep—Fiction. 3. Animals—Fiction. 4. Stories in rhyme] I. Title.   PZ8.3.B7Go   1985   [E]   85-2098   ISBN: 0-394-87285-1 (trade); 0-394-97285-6 (lib. bdg.)

Manufactured in the United States of America   1 2 3 4 5 6 7 8 9 0

GOOD NIGHT

Based on *The Going to Bed Book*

by Sandra Boynton

Random House New York

The sun has set
not long ago.

Now everybody

to take a bath
in one big tub
with soap all over—
SCRUB SCRUB SCRUB.

They hang their towels
on the wall

and find pajamas,

big
and
small.

With some on top
and some beneath,
they brush and brush
and brush their teeth.

And when the moon is

on the rise, they all go up

to exercise!

And down once more,
but not so fast,
they're on their way
to bed at last.

They climb into
their feather bed—

some at the foot,

some at the head.

Two little rabbits
sing a song

while everybody
hums along:

Allegretto

The hip - pos, big hip - pos, will dance in the mud, the pig - gies will fol - low them in;

and down in that hol - low will el - e-phants wal - low in mud that comes up to the chin!

The cats and the bears, the li-ons and dogs, the rhi-no and moose come a-long;

ritard

Two rab-bits (that's we two) will glad-ly a-gree to sing ev-'ry-one's dream in a song!

The day is done.
They say good night,
and somebody
turns off the light.

The moon is high,

the sea is deep—

they rock

and rock

and rock

to sleep.